Sedric

AND THE
ROMAN HOLIDAY RAMPAGE

First published in Great Britain 2016
by Jelly Pie an imprint of Egmont UK Ltd
The Yellow Building, 1 Nicholas Road, London W11 4AN

Text and illustration copyright © Angie Morgan 2016
The moral rights of the author—illustrator have been asserted.

ISBN 978 1 4052 8283 3

www.egmont.co.uk

A CIP catalogue record for this title is available from the British Library

Printed and bound in Great Britain by the CPI Group

64121/1

Stay safe online. Any website addresses listed in this book are correct at the time of going to
print. However, Egmont is not responsible for content hosted by third parties. Please be aware
that online content can be subject to change and websites can contain content that is unsuitable
for children. We advise that all children are supervised when using the internet.

Sedric

AND THE
ROMAN HOLIDAY RAMPAGE

Angie Morgan

Little Soggy in the Mud
The Dark Ages - about 600AD'ish (I think)

Dear Reader

I've written another book about me and my
friends who live in our tiny small village
that is down in the bottom left hand bit of
Britain where it goes all pointy. We get up to
all sorts of exciting and dangerous stuff
with some new characters, and the nasty and
slimey toad, Baron Dennis, and his greedy fat
wife Prunehilda (who both totally **HATE** us)
still live in the castle. I recently heard a rumour
that they were going on a Mediterranean
cruise to **ROME** *

        But I will say no more as you're probably
itching to start the story, but before you do
please read the NEXT PAGES just in case you
haven't read my other books OR you've read
one but it was AGES ago and you've forgotten
who everyone is or....

                    Turn over page ➝

The CASTLE

BARON DENNIS

who is totally HORRIBLE and MEAN

PRUNEHILDA

Greedy and pointless wife of DENNIS

MUCUS

Dennis and Prunehilda's manky and stuck up son

SINUS

Mucus's best (also stuck up) friend

SERGEANT HENGIST

Who is in charge of the castle

ROGER and **NORMAN**

our friends (who tell us stuff about what Dennis is up to)

Chapter One

MUD, STICKS AND QUITE A LOT OF SHOUTING

'That **TOTALLY** does it! I'm going to leave this pointless stinkin' mud-soaked borin' village where nothin' ever happens!' shouted Rubella. 'And I'm goin' to go somewhere where there aren't **STUPID** people who hit other people in the face with sacks of mud!'

Rubella (all CROSS)

1

Rubella was overreacting a bit, if you ask me. It was only a SMALL sack of mud and Urk hadn't thrown it VERY hard.

'Sorry, Rubella,' shouted Urk, 'but this game is totally AWESOME!'

'Oh my days! How can throwing a sack of mud and hitting it with a stick be awesome?' yelled Rubella.

'Maybe we could make it more interesting if the person with the stick tried to run really fast between two trees or something while the other person tried to catch the sack of mud?' said my best friend Verucca.

Eg thought it was a stupid idea, but that some sort of protective hat might be useful.

PROTECTIVE HAT

Rubella said that ALL our ideas were totally stupid, but that this one won the stupid prize in a competition for most stupid thing EVER in a whole world full of stupid stuff.

'Why don't you go away, then?' said Verucca, 'instead of hanging round here MOANING all the time?'

Rubella looked SO cross, I wondered if she was actually going to explode.

'Right, Verucca Stupidface – I will! But you'll be sorry when I'm gone, because one day I'll come back and I'll be all rich and wearing fancy clothes

and jewellery and then you'll wish you'd been nicer to me. You coming, Gert?' she shouted as she got ready for a big flounce-off.*

'Bye, Urk,' mumbled Gert (which was weird as she never normally says ANYTHING).

'Bye, Gert,' said Urk quietly, giving a tiny wave.

We all stared at Urk, who went bright red right down to his neck.

URK going red →

'WHAT?' he said. 'There's something on my face isn't there? Why are you all staring at me?'

*
To Flounce off: (verb)
The act of walking
and being grumpy
at the same time.

Chapter Two

IN WHICH SERGEANT HENGIST IS FRIENDLY
(WHICH IS A BIT WEIRD AND WORRYING)

After Rubella and Gert left, Sergeant Hengist arrived with Roger and Norman. They're guards who work for the baron in the castle and they're well nice. We waved a cheery hello to them and Sergeant Hengist waved back, which was weird. He'd never done before.

Sergeant Hengist works for the baron too and there are some important facts about him that you need to know:

1. He's a very ANGRY man and he shouts ALL the time, and when he's not shouting or asleep he's complaining about us.

2. Sometimes when he gets angry one of his eyes spins round and round, which looks weird and a bit scary.

3. He totally hates us because he's always plotting stuff with the baron, but we find out what his plans are and ruin them.

'Right, you two,' he said (being smiley and strangely UN-shouty for some reason) to Roger and Norman. 'I want you to lay these sacks all along the track leading from the village. We don't want his lordship's chariot getting stuck in the mud or anything, do we?'

'No, sarge,' said Roger.

'That would be a disaster, wouldn't it, sarge?'
agreed Norman.

'Are you being sarcastic, corporal?' said the
sergeant.

'Me? No, sarge!' said Norman. 'I just meant that
you've really been looking forward to this holiday thing,
haven't you?'

'And we don't know what sarcastic means, do we,
Norm?' added Roger.

'Sorry boys, it's just that I'm a bit tense. I keep thinking that something might go wrong,' he said.

'What could POSSIBLY go wrong, sarge?' said Norman. 'Everything's going to be just fine. You've done all your packing, and put in all your clothes for the lovely HOT weather, haven't you? You just leave everything to me and Rog.'

'Thanks, boys. And you're right. Everything is going

to be just FINE,' said the sergeant happily, and as he headed back towards the castle he did a little skip and made a strange growling noise. I THINK it was him singing.

'What's wrong with HIM?' said Verucca as soon as he was out of earshot. 'Has he had a bump on the head or something?'

'Haven't you heard?' said Norman.

'Heard what?' I asked.

'His lordship the baron and his wife Prunehilda, and their two posh friends, Boris and Lucretia, are going off on some sort of a holiday – I think it's called a cruise or something – to ROME,' said Roger. 'The sarge is quite excited. He's been looking forward to it for AGES.'

'What's a cruise?' said Urk.

'I'm not sure,' said Roger slowly, 'but I think it involves a boat of some sort and maybe some water?'

'So, why is the sergeant excited?' I said. 'Is he going too?'

'He is,' said Roger. 'He's going along to help the baron and his wife with stuff. He's never had a holiday before, what with him working day and night for his lordship for so long. The singing thing's been a bit weird, but it's been lovely seeing him so happy, hasn't it, Norm?'

'Lovely, Rog. He hasn't been this happy since Mrs Hengist left him. He did the singing thing then, too.'

After Roger and Norman had gone off with their sacks, we heard a rumbling noise in the distance. As it got closer it got louder and louder until suddenly a horse and cart came galloping out of the trees, heading straight for us.

We threw ourselves out of the way just in time. The cart went rumbling past, and as it did, two boys in very fancy clothes stuck their heads out of the back of it, sniggering and pointing at us.

'Oh my sainted trousers, Sinus!' shouted one of them, who had totally enormous teeth. 'What ARE they doing, lying in the mud?'

'It's probably a peasant thing,' said the other boy.

'WE'RE IN THE MUD BECAUSE YOU NEARLY RAN US OVER!' I shouted furiously.

'What did he say, Mucus?' said the other boy.

'Not a clue!' snorted the first one, whose laugh sounded like a cross between a donkey and a pig. 'It's probably some strange PEASANT language or something!'

Then, as the cart turned towards the hill leading up to castle, the wheels hit a bump. The two boys screamed and clutched the sides of the cart.

11

'There's NO WAY that cart is getting up the hill,' Urk mumbled from the mud.

US lying in mud.

After they'd disappeared from sight, we heard a shrill angry voice shouting, 'WHAT DO YOU MEAN, WE'RE STUCK?! I'M NOT WALKING ALL THE WAY UP THAT HILL!'

'Told you,' sniggered Urk.

'We need to find out who those boys are,' said Verucca as we picked ourselves up and headed off to school, 'and what on earth they're doing here.'

'Let's ask Gaius,' I said.

Chapter Three

RUMOURS OF RICH BOYS

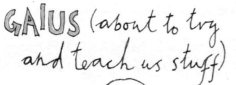

GAIUS (about to try and teach us stuff)

Gaius, our teacher, is Roman. He's also **REALLY** old and **WELL** clever. He stayed here when all the other Romans went back to Rome because he said that Rome was too hot and everyone smelled of garlic, and he started a school in our village to try to teach us stuff.

He sometimes actually manages it.

When we arrived at school he looked us up and down and frowned. We were VERY muddy. Gaius has a special way of frowning that makes you feel really guilty without him even having to say anything.

'I trust you all have a good reason for turning up to school late AND looking like you've been rolling in the pigsty?' he said.

'We've just had a brush with death, sir,' said Robin darkly, as Denzel sneaked through the door behind Gaius and hid himself under a bench.

'Oh, dear. That does sound rather alarming, Robin. Do tell me more . . .' said Gaius without turning round, '. . . AFTER Sedric has removed his pig from my classroom.'

14

I've never worked out how Gaius does that. He says he's got eyes in the back of his head, but I don't think he does really.

So, after I'd taken Denzel outside, we told Gaius all about the two posh boys in the cart.

'Who do you think they were, sir?' said Verucca.

'Well,' said Gaius, 'I do remember hearing a rumour that the baron and Prunehilda have a son, who's away in a boarding school somewhere I believe. One of the boys could possibly have been him.'

'Imagine a school filled with boys like THAT,' said Robin. 'They most probably have special lessons to teach them how to look down their noses at the downtrodden poor.'

HOW TO BE POSH LESSON

Nose for looking down

Sneer

Robin sometimes gets a bit worked up about the 'downtrodden poor', which I think is us, mostly.

'That may be true, Robin,' said Gaius. 'But just because the rich have more money it doesn't necessarily make them better than us.'

'What are you talking about, sir?' asked Rubella, who had just arrived with Gert trailing behind her.

'We believe that the baron and Prunehilda's son and his friend have recently arrived at the castle, Rubella dear. But it's only a rumour,' said Gaius. 'Now, I would like you all to sit down, while I take the register.'

Rubella looked Very Interested, which was unusual because her usual look was Bored, Fed Up And Angry. Gert sat next to Urk, who went bright red again, and Rubella had to sit next to Verucca because it was the only space left. She wasn't happy about it, though.

'Not living in a great big CASTLE yet, then?' grinned Verucca.

'Oh, very funny, Verucca Stupidface!' snapped Rubella. 'You think you're WELL clever, don't you?'

'Girls. No arguing please,' said Gaius quickly. 'I WOULD like to start the geography lesson if it's not TOO much to ask.'

Gaius knew that Rubella and Verucca could argue for totally hours if he didn't stop them. I sometimes wondered what would happen if no one DID stop them. Maybe they'd both explode or catch fire or something?

So Gaius droned on about geography, which is his second favourite subject after Roman history. He told us all about a big sea with a long name beginning with M* that he said Baron Dennis and Prunehilda would have to cross on their cruise, and then he told us some other stuff about people called PIRATES, who are basically just OUTLAWS in boats.

* MEDITERRANEAN CRUISE -
Which is when people go across the Mediterranean
(it that is lovely warm blue sea) in a big boat ship
and eat and drink far too much on the way while
also trying to avoid PIRATES.

They sounded **WELL** cool.

But then, while Robin and Eg were handing out the twigs and mud for handwriting practice, Gaius fell asleep. He does this a lot, due to being so incredibly **OLD**, so we left him snoring and all tiptoed outside.

Rubella was first out of the door, which was weird,

Rubell

because she's usually really slow. She thinks walking's well boring. But today she set off really fast towards the castle, with Gert running after her to keep up.

We knew she was going to spy on the posh boys, so we followed her.

US tiptoeing out

ing REALLY fast (unusual)

Chapter Four

A DISAPPOINTMENT FOR SERGEANT HENGIST

Rubella was WELL annoyed with us for following her. She shouted at us ALL the way up the hill, so we ignored her, which annoyed her even more.

When we reached the top of the hill, we hid behind a bush. We didn't want anyone to see us because we weren't very popular in the castle. Rubella had to squeeze behind the bush with us because it was the best bush for spying and that made her even MORE grumpy. Urk told her she looked like an angry hornet (which also didn't help).

Dennis and Prunehilda and their friends Boris and Lucretia were all standing outside the castle with the two boys from before. Sergeant Hengist was there too, sorting out piles of bags and loading them on to the baron's chariot.

'Of course it's LOVELY to see you, Mucus Dahling!' Prunehilda said to the one with the enormous teeth, giving him a big slobbery kiss. 'But you should have let us know you were coming home!'

'Yuk!' whispered Eg. 'Imagine being kissed by HER!' Urk sniggered and made a gagging noise.

'I hope your explanation for turning up unexpectedly and spoiling our plans is an extremely good one, Mucus,' said Dennis, angrily.

'Well, it's a bit – er – complicated, father,' said Mucus, smirking and looking at Sinus.

'Yes, sir,' Sinus said quickly. 'It is. VERY

complicated INDEED and a bit –
er – UNEXPECTED.'

'What ARE you blathering on
about, boy?' shouted Boris. 'Sinus, I
sometimes wonder why I pay all that money for your
education when all you seem to do is talk rubbish!'

Sinus looked at Mucus.

'Well,' said Mucus, slowly. 'Old Stinker, the
headmaster, suddenly decided that we'd all been SO –
er – incredibly GOOD and WELL-BEHAVED
and everything that he'd give us a special holiday. He
said to say he's REALLY
sorry but he sort
of didn't have
time to let the
parents know . . .'
'SPECIAL
HOLIDAY!' shouted

Mucus

Sinus

OLD STINKER (the Headmaster) with hair on fire.

Dennis, turning a strange purpléy colour. 'Do you think I was born yesterday? St Ghastly's doesn't DO holidays. That's why we send you there. You've been EXPELLED, haven't you?! Did you set fire to the headmaster's hair again, or was it something WORSE this time?'

'Now, Dennis – it did grow back, and he wasn't VERY cross,' said Prunehilda.

'WASN'T VERY CROSS?' spluttered Dennis. 'He only promised not to expel the boy after I paid him a huge amount of money and bought him a WIG!' yelled Dennis.

'We're AWFULLY sorry,' said the boys, who didn't look sorry at all.

'Well I'm NOT giving up my cruise,' said Lucretia. 'I'm all packed and ready. You'll just have to go back to school, Sinus!'

Sinus handed his father a piece of parchment.

'You need to read this, father,' he said, nervously.

Boris's face darkened.

'I DON'T BELIEVE IT! IT SAYS HERE THAT THEY CAN'T GO BACK! THE HEADMASTER HAS GONE COMPLETELY INSANE AND THE TEACHERS HAVE HAD TO LOCK HIM UP!'

'We could always stay here in the castle, father,' said Mucus, innocently. 'Sergeant Hengist can stay and look after us.'

Sergeant Hengist went white.

'Oh no, please, sire. I'm all packed, and I've been rather looking forward to the holiday – and I REALLY haven't got those sorts of skills,' he said.

He looked like a starving man who had just sat down to eat a lovely meal and then found that some rats had got there first and it had all gone. 'I'm sure the boys would LOVE to come on the cruise with us – all that sea air and everything. Isn't sea air supposed to be good for – um – boys?'

'Nonsense, man!' the baron said. 'You don't REALLY need to come with us. You'll probably be seasick or get sunstroke or something. No, this is the perfect solution. The boys can stay here in the castle with YOU, and WE can go off on our cruise.'

'You'll all have SUCH fun together!' squawked Prunehilda gaily.

Sinus and Mucus glanced at Sergeant Hengist, who now looked like the rats had finished eating his lovely meal and were now munching on his feet.

RATS munching Sergeant Hengist's dinner.

'We'll be fine with Sergeant Hengist,' said Mucus slyly. 'As long as he does as he's told.'

'A chip off the old block, eh, Hengist?' laughed Dennis, slapping the sergeant on the back.

Sergeant Hengist opened his mouth to speak, but no words came out.

No words →

Chapter Five

MY MUM, SOME RATS AND AN AWFUL LOT OF SHOUTING

As we crept back down the hill to the village I went over all the stuff we had found out about the posh boys.

1. Mucus was DEFINITELY the son of Dennis and Prunehilda, and Sinus was Boris and Lucretia's son. They were ALSO both complete twonks.

2. They seemed VERY keen to be left behind in the castle. (Why?)

3, They had been expelled for something SO bad it had driven their headmaster bonkers.

4, They had REALLY annoying voices.

Rubella was WELL impressed, though. She said that even if Mucus did seem a bit of a chinless twonk, he was VERY rich, so she was willing to overlook small details.

Verucca was disgusted with Rubella and spent the walk back to the village telling her exactly HOW disgusted she was, but when we got there she stopped because we could hear my mum screaming.

There are lots of reasons why my mum screams, but mostly it means she's found a rat.

My mum's terrified of rats. When she finds one in our hovel (which is pretty much every day) she goes completely mental. She bashes about with the broom and

shouts at my dad, as if it's **HIS** fault that the village
is full of rats, which is unfair, because it's not.

My mum finding RAT

'Don't just stand there, Wilfred! Can't you
do something useful, like make some rat traps or
something?!' screamed my mum.

'FLAPJACKS?' shouted Eg's grandad, who's
as deaf as a tree.

'DID SOMEBODY MENTION FLAPJACKS?'

Flapjack

'She said RAT TRAPS, not FLAPJACKS, Grandad!' said Eg.

Rat-trap

'I KNOW, I'M NOT DEAF!' shouted Eg's grandad. 'I'LL HAVE MINE WITH A NICE CUP OF TURNIP TEA.'

'Calm down, Ethel,' pleaded my dad. 'You've already broken our best chair AND bashed a hole in the wall.'

I've found that telling my mum to calm down usually makes her do the opposite, so she just screamed louder and took another wild swing with her broom. She actually managed to hit a tiny rat that was standing too close to the door.

'I've got an idea, Sedric's mum,' said Verucca kindly, taking the broom out of her hand. 'Why don't you go to our hovel and have a rest? My mum'll make you a nice cup of turnip tea.'

'Oh, thank you, Verucca love,' said my mum weakly, as Verucca led her away.

After they'd gone, I picked up the tiny rat. It was limp and dead-looking.

'I don't think it's dead, Sedric,' whispered a small voice by my elbow. 'I can see its chest moving up and down.'

It was Verucca's little brother, Burp.

'Me and Vlad'll make it better,' he said, as he gently took the rat from my hand and put it into his pocket, before heading off towards the pigsty.

Burp's best friend Vlad lives in the pigsty. Before he came to the village,

Tiny broken rat

he used to be called Vlad the Bad, and we all thought he was a dangerous head—chopping criminal, but then we found out that the baron and Sergeant Hengist had told lies about him and he wasn't bad at all. He's actually really kind and gentle. He looks WELL scary, though, like all his family, who ARE mostly outlaws and generally BAD people.

Vlad and Burp became best friends because they both love looking after injured animals and stuff, and the pigsty became a sort of animal hospital, filled with every sort of sick creature they could find.

They have quite a lot.

Chapter Six

TURNIPS AND TANTRUMS

Gaius was just waking up when we got back to school, so we told him what we'd found out about the posh boys, then he made us do some handwriting and adding up, and then school ended so we went off to the turnip field to play our new game.

On the way Urk said, 'I've just had a BRILLIANT idea. We could stick three sticks in the ground and balance a little stick on top, then we throw mud balls at the stick and a person with a big stick tries to bat them away.

We could call it. . . "Sticket" or something. What do you think?'

We all said it was an awesome idea. Robin said he liked the name, seeing as it was very much a stick-based game. Rubella said that it was STILL stupid and pointless and that she and Gert had something MUCH better to do.

'What? Like looking for Mucus? You're wasting your time, you know,' said Verucca. 'He's much too snobby to look at YOU! He'll most probably end up marrying some rich girl with a posh voice who isn't all covered in mud because she

Posh girl having a bath

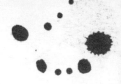

spends all her time having BATHS!'

'I can have baths TOO, Verucca Stupidface. I've just not had one YET!' said Rubella angrily.

They were still arguing when we reached the edge of the turnip field and something round and muddy hit Eg on the head.

'OW! URK! We haven't started playing yet, and if you're going to hit THAT hard, I think we need to work on the protective hat thing!' said Eg.

'That weren't me!' said Urk.

Then something hit me on the head too. It was a turnip.

'I SAY!' shouted an annoying voice. 'I THINK I HIT ONE! THIS IS MUCH MORE FUN THAN ST GHASTLY'S! SHALL I SEE IF I CAN HIT ANOTHER ONE?'

It was Mucus and Sinus. They were squelching

across the field towards us, hurling more turnips. One hit Denzel.

'I GOT THE PIG!' squealed Mucus. 'This is totes excellent fun! It's even BETTER than that time we hung the little

ticks from Lower School out of the windows and pelted them with bread rolls!'

'HEY!' I shouted. **'STOP HITTING MY PIG! THIS IS OUR FIELD AND YOU NEED TO GET OFF IT!'**

'I SAY!' shouted Mucus. **'DO YOU PEASANTS KNOW WHO I AM?'**

'No.' I lied. I wasn't going to let him know we'd been spying on them.

'I am Mucus,' he said, squelching nearer and pulling himself up to his full size, which wasn't very big. 'I am Baron Dennis's son. My father owns EVERYTHING around here, so you'd better watch how you speak to me or you'll end up in serious trouble!'

'He doesn't own this field. It's OURS!' I shouted back.

'No. I don't think you understand,' said Mucus airily. 'You're PEASANTS and peasants don't OWN fields.'

'Well, we ARE peasants, but it's OUR field and they're OUR turnips!' said Verucca. 'The old Baron, Osric, gave them to us.'

'The old Baron?' said Mucus, looking confused. 'Sorry. You've TOTALLY lost me. And what in Hades are turnips?'

Turnip

'Ignore them, Mucus. They're just spoiling our fun,' said Sinus, as he threw another turnip in our direction.

'OW!' said Eg, as the turnip bounced off his nose. 'That REALLY hurt!'

'Look what you've done!' I said, as Eg's nose began to drip blood. (Eg has EPIC nosebleeds.) 'Now will you STOP throwing our turnips around?'

'Oh THESE are turnips are they?' said Mucus.

Eg's nose bleeding (epic)

'I didn't know they had a name. What exactly are they
FOR?'

'We EAT them,' said Verucca, as Sinus hurled
another one and hit Denzel again. He squealed and hid
behind my legs.

'No way!' said Mucus, giggling. 'No one could possibly
EAT these – they're just lumps of MUD!'

'Well, we DO eat them actually, and you need to
stop throwing them. You've really hurt Denzel,' I said.

'Oh cripes! The pig has a name too!' said Mucus.
'That is SO lame! I suppose it lives with you in your
smelly little shed thing and sleeps in your bed!'

The two boys sniggered some more, which made Verucca go REALLY red-in-the-face angry. I reckoned she had two choices. She could either,

1. Punch Mucus and feel a MILLION times better before getting into a massive amount of trouble.

2. Ignore Mucus and walk away and avoid getting into a massive amount of trouble, but also NOT feel a million times better.

I was secretly hoping that a huge troll would come crashing out of the Dark Forest and carry them both away, which would be totally BRILLIANT but was unlikely. But it turned out she didn't need to do anything because Mucus took one look at her angry red face and he backed away screaming, 'DON'T YOU COME NEAR ME! I MEAN IT!

TROLL

DON'T YOU DARE HURT ME! I'LL
TELL MUMMY AND YOU'LL PROBABLY
BE THROWN IN THE DUNGEONS
OR SOMETHING WHERE YOU'LL
STARVE TO DEATH OR-OR- BE

TORTURED WITH HOT SPIKY THINGS! HENGIST! HELP!! WE'RE BEING ATTACKED BY WILD PEASANTS AND THEY'RE ACTUALLY GOING TO KILL US!'

He really was a MASSIVE wimp.

Chapter Seven

WiMPS AND WiLD PEASANTS
(AND SOME WHOPPING GREAT LIES)

Then, as Mucus was STILL screaming at Verucca,
Rubella suddenly strolled between them and gazed up
at Mucus from under a curtain of hair.

'Hi, Mucus. My name's Rubella,' she whispered.

Mucus stopped screaming. His mouth dropped open and his eyes went all staring and goggly. He looked like a small frightened rabbit does when it's faced with a very large and hungry fox.

Small frightened rabbit

Very hungry fox

'What's wrong with him? Why's he looking at Rubella like that?' whispered Eg.

'He probably fancies her,' said Urk.

'Don't be daft. He'd have to be WELL weird to fancy HER,' said Eg. 'Do you think he knows how grumpy she is?'

Then I noticed Denzel.

He was tiptoeing round behind the two posh boys,
who were still backing away from Verucca and Rubella.
When he got just behind Mucus and Sinus's legs, he
stood quite still and waited until they reached him, and
they tripped and fell backwards, landing with two loud
splats in the mud.

DENZEL
doing GOOD
(using stealth)

There was a long silence, like the silence that
usually happens just before an awful lot of loud stuff,
then . . .

'HENGIIIST!!' screamed Mucus.

'HELP! I'M DYING IS THAT BLOOD OH MY VELVET UNDERPANTS I'M BLEEDING! HENGIIIIIIST! WHERE ARE YOU? GET ME OUT OF HERE NOW!!!!'

Sergeant Hengist's very own cloud of misery

'It's not **YOUR** blood – it's mine. Look,' said Eg, and he leaned over Mucus and dripped more of his nose blood on to him.

'AARRGGHH! GROSS!' screamed Mucus in horror.

The sergeant appeared at last, trudging miserably across the field towards us.

'HENGIST! WHERE IN HADES

46

HAVE YOU BEEN?' shouted Mucus. 'How DARE you ignore me when I shout? These – these FILTHY peasants attacked us for TOTES no reason! Sinus and I were innocently picking wild flowers when they just went for us, like animals. Don't just stand there looking stupid, Hengist! Get us OUT of here!'

'That is such a LIE!' I shouted. 'You started it. YOU threw the turnips at US!'

'Do we LOOK like turnip throwers? I mean, REALLY?' said Mucus, as Hengist pulled him out of the mud with a sound like a cork coming out of a bottle.

'We'd best get you back to the castle and cleaned up then, young sirs,' said the sergeant with a sigh.

'Bye, Mucus,' whispered Rubella.

Mucus's eyes went all glazed again, and he stared open-mouthed at Rubella as Sergeant Hengist led him and Sinus unsteadily back across the field towards the castle.

Chapter Eight

PARCHMENT, POSTS AND MYSTERIOUS WRITING

After that none of us felt much like playing Sticket,

so we headed back over

the bridge towards

the village.

Plus Eg's nose was STILL bleeding and he'd used up all our rags and hankies mopping up the blood, so we needed to get some more. Verucca said she was getting a bit bored with the whole hitting sacks of mud with sticks thing anyway. Urk said she was insane as it was the best thing ever invented since someone invented the very first best thing ever.

'It's not that I don't LIKE hitting things with sticks, it's just that I think there might be more to life,' said Verucca.

I told her she sounded like Rubella.

Rubella sniggered and Verucca glared at me, then we saw Roger and Norman. They were carrying some wooden posts and a hammer and they waved at us, so we went over.

When I asked them how things were going up at the castle, they looked a bit fed up.

Roger and Norman being GLOOMY

'It's not good,' said Roger gloomily. 'It's all gone downhill since those boys arrived. They've got NO manners, and poor Sergeant Hengist is SO depressed about missing his holiday that he can't even be bothered to shout any more. The guards have stopped guarding stuff, and the sarge doesn't seem to notice. Me and Norm said it's all going to end very badly if something isn't done, didn't we, Norm?'

'We did say that, Rog,' said Norman, and they both stared off into the distance, looking miserable.

I didn't know what to say, so I asked them what the wooden posts were for.

'That's a good question, isn't it, Norm?' said Roger.

'Yes, Rog,' said Norman, 'and it's a question we asked ourselves, isn't it?'

'We did, Norm,' said Roger.

'Did you get an answer?' said Eg.

'No, we didn't,' said Norman. 'That Mucus and his

friend just told us to hammer the posts in the ground along the track leading from the village and some other places. No explanation or nothing.'

'So they didn't tell you to do anything else, except bang some posts into the ground? That doesn't make any sense.'

'Oh, there was something else,' said Roger. 'I nearly forgot. Young Mucus gave us these and said to nail them to the posts, didn't he, Norm?'

Roger pulled some crumpled bits of parchment from his pocket.

'He did, Rog,' said Norman. 'I remember his exact words. He said it's "totally the latest way to communicate".'

'Let's have a look, then,' said Verucca. Roger handed her one. It said:

Totes mega
Castyle Rave

This weekend
Lolz ☺
from Mucus & Sinus

Blob of ~~pickle~~
apple sauce

'What's that blob on the bottom?' I said.

'I think it's pickle,' said Roger. He stuck his finger in and tasted it. 'No. I tell a lie. It's apple sauce.'

'I told you not to put the parchments in the same pocket as your lunch, Rog,' said Norman. 'They're all messy now.'

'What's it mean, though?' said Robin.

'Don't ask me,' said Roger, as he started banging a post into the ground.

'It's got to mean SOMETHING,' said Urk.

'Everything's got to mean something.'

'Not always,' said Eg. 'My grandad says a lot of stuff that doesn't mean ANYTHING.'

'That's because he's deaf as a stick and he always hears things wrong,' said Eg.

'It sounds like Mucus and Sinus are planning to do something in the castle. It says "this weekend" – which is tomorrow,' said Verucca. 'Don't know what "totes mega" or "rave" mean though.'

Totes mega Castle Rave This weekend Lolz :" from Mucus & Sinus

Roger finished banging the post in and Norman nailed one of the bits of parchment to it.

'Well, we'd best be going,' said Roger. 'Got to put the rest of these posts up.'

'One thing's definite,' said Norman. 'It's all going to end badly. VERY badly indeed.'

Chapter Nine

RA RA RA FOR ST GHASTLY'S!
(LOL)

The next morning was Saturday and we woke to cold drizzly rain and no school, so we set off to play a game of Sticket at the edge of the turnip field. But as we crossed the track leading out of the village we heard the sound of carts approaching, and some heehawing noises that sounded horribly like Mucus and Sinus.

Drizzly rain (That's rain that doesn't FALL. It just sort of hangs about)

It wasn't them though. It was lots of boys who looked and sounded EXACTLY like them.

They arrived in all sorts of carts and carriages driven by servants and pulled by horses and mules of every size and colour, and which owing to the drizzle, had all got stuck in the mud as soon as they reached the bottom of the hill.

There was a LOT of complaining when the posh boys realised they had to get down and walk. You'd have thought they'd never SEEN mud before.

Posh boys wobbling

And while they were complaining, Mucus and Sinus arrived. Mucus was all pink and excited. '**HEY!** You guys! It's SO cool you made it! We're going to have the best time $EVER!$' he shouted.

'Where's this "mega rave" thing of yours, Mukester? Hope it's not in those horrid little sheds over there!' sniggered a boy with curly blond hair who was wobbling unsteadily in the mud and pointing at our hovels.

'Haha! No way! That's where the stinking peasants live. The party's in the castle up there. It's actually MINE,' Mucus said smugly. 'The parents have gone away on their hols, so we can TOTES do whatever we want.'

'Awesome!' said the curly-haired boy.

Mucus's friends seemed to find everything screamingly funny and laughed like donkeys, apart from one who snorted like a pig, which made Denzel all

OINK!

Denzel and friend

OINK!

excited because he thought he'd found a friend.

Mucus went around saying 'Hi!' a lot and telling everyone how cool everything was and what a totes MEGA time they were all going to have because it was basically HIS castle now. After he'd said it enough times I think he really convinced himself it was true.

'Sergeant Hengist is going to go totally MENTAL when he finds out Mucus is having a party in the castle,' said Eg.

'If he hasn't gone mental already,' said Urk. 'He was looking WELL weird last time we saw him.'

'I felt a bit sorry for him,' said Verucca.

'How can you feel sorry for him after all the horrible things he's done to us?' said Robin.

'Well, no one's ALL bad,' said Verucca.

'Sergeant Hengist is,' said Urk.

'It's so unfair. He'd been looking forward

to his holiday, and then it all
went wrong and he got lumbered
with looking after stupid Mucus and
his stupid friend,' said Verucca,
as Mucus and his friends passed us.

Mucus glared at us.

'Ignore the peasants, chaps.
They're AWFULLY rough and
stupid, and they're so NOT
invited to my total MEGA
LEGEND of a party . . .' he
said, and then he stopped and his
eyes went all weirdly goggly again.

Rubella was leaning against
a tree and fiddling with
her hair.

Rubella (who is actually a GIR]
and therefore so NOT invited
to castle party.)

'Hi, Mucus! Am I invited to your party, then?' she said.

'I, er – gosh – er, well, um . . .' he stammered.

'I didn't know you were inviting GIRLS to this castle bash of yours,' said the one with curly hair.

'And didn't you just say the peasants were all a bit ROUGH, Mucus?' said a large one with rosy cheeks.

'Yes – um – they certainly ARE! No peasants OR girls at MY party – no way!' Mucus stammered.

'OK, CHAPS! Let's PARTY!' shouted Sinus, as they all squelched through the mud, honking and snorting up the hill to the castle.

Rubella watched them go with a murderous look in her eye.

Rubella's DEATH STARE
(You should probably turn the page now...)

'See. I told you he didn't fancy her,' whispered Eg.
'He probably found out how grumpy she is.'

Chapter Ten

SAVAGE BEASTS AND AWFUL SINGING

The noise from the party in the castle got louder and louder, and by dusk all the grown-ups in the village had had enough, so they all went inside and shut their doors.

We played Sticket until it was too dark to see and then we sat under the Old Oak Tree.

'Do you reckon we could teach other people how to play Sticket? It might spread all round the world and then we'd be famous,' said Urk.

'Don't see why not,' said Eg. 'It's definitely the best game we've ever invented.'

'It's the ONLY game you've invented,' said Verucca.

'There's Sticks and Stones,' said Robin. 'We invented that.'

STICKS AND STONES
The Rules

You will need: 2 players (or more. Actually you can have as many as you want. The rules are quite ~~flexible~~ vague.)

You will also need...

1. A stick
2. A stone

Player 1 hits the stone with stick. It will most probably land in the mud, so while he/she is looking for it, Player 2 hits his/her stone with his/her stick.

~~When~~ If Player 1 finds their stone he/she can hit it again...etc. etc.

The game is over when the players get bored of looking for their stones.

64

'What? That pointless thing where you just hit stones with sticks into mud?' said Rubella. 'That's not really a game is it?'

'Listen,' said Eg. 'The posh boys are getting REALLY loud.'

Eg was right. The noise was REALLY loud.

'It sounds as if they're coming down the hill,' said Robin.

'Why would they want to do that?' said Eg.

'No idea,' said Robin.

But they were. The posh boys were coming down the hill towards the village, and they were singing.

'WE ARE THE BOYS FROM ST GHASTLY'S SCHOOL!
WE'RE RICH AND RATHER LOUD,
WE'RE MEGA POSH AND

REAAHLLY COOL
        SING RA FOR THE
GHASTLY'S CROWD!'

It was loud and tuneless, so
we put our fingers in our ears until
they reached the village, where they
stopped singing and squelched about, snorting
and giggling in the dark and bumping into things.

'What are we actually DOING here, Mucus? It's
AWFULLY muddy!' squeaked a voice from the dark.

'Thought we'd pay Daddy's peasants a visit,' said
Mucus. 'It'll be SUCH a laugh because they're all
REALLY stupid!'

'But there don't seem to be any peasants here!
Are they all on holiday or something?' someone shouted.

'I don't think they have holidays,' shouted Mucus. 'They're MUCH too poor and stupid.'

'I SAY!' came another voice. 'DO THEY ACTUALLY LIVE IN THESE TINY SHED THINGS? THEY MUST BE AWFULLY SMALL!'

Then a turnip hit the school roof and Sinus shouted from the direction of the turnip store. 'Try this, chaps! It's EPIC fun! The peasants call them TURNIPS and – you SO won't believe this – they actually EAT them!'

There were howls of laughter as another turnip hit our hovel roof. I heard my mum scream, and then turnips were flying everywhere, bouncing off roofs and trees and hitting walls. Someone found our cart and pulled it round and round the village, bashing into hovels and knocking down fences.

'We have to stop them!' said Verucca.

'They're breaking our village!'

'But how?' I said. 'There are loads of them and it's too dark to see anything!'

'And someone could get seriously hurt,' said Eg nervously.

'OW!' shouted Urk as a turnip hit him on the head.

Then another turnip flew out of the darkness and hit Denzel.

He looked VERY cross. He narrowed his little piggy eyes and glanced up at me before racing off into the darkness.

'Stop him, Sedric!' shouted Verucca. 'He might get hurt!'

'AARRGGHH! THERE'S A WILD ANIMAL LOOSE!' shouted someone.

'IT'S OVER HERE! WHAT IS IT?'

'UUGGHH! I FELT ITS HORRIBLE WET NOSE!'

'OH, MY SAINTED UNDERPANTS IT'S GOT ME TOO!' yelled Mucus. 'W·W·WHAT IS IT? HENGIST! WHERE ARE YOU, YOU STUPID MAN? THERE'S A HERD OF SAVAGE BEASTS ON THE LOOSE AND THEY'RE ACTUALLY EATING US.

MUMMY WILL BE LIVID WITH YOU IF SHE COMES BACK AND FINDS I'VE BEEN EATEN!'

There was a LOT of screaming from the terrified posh boys, as they ran around panicking and bumping into each other. It seemed to go on for AGES until Roger and Norman appeared out of the darkness, carrying flaming torches and followed by the shambling figure of Sergeant Hengist, who was wearing a toga (weird) and a strangely vacant expression.

'There you are, Hengist! Where in Hades have you been?' yelled Mucus furiously. 'Mummy said you had to look after me ALL the time!'

'That's no way to talk to the sergeant, young sire,' said Roger calmly. 'Now, where are these savage beasts you claim were attacking you?'

'What do you mean, CLAIM? They WERE attacking us! They were HUGE, with big bitey teeth and claws and everything!' shouted Mucus.

Norman waved his torch about. 'Well, they all seem to be gone now, sire. There's nothing but this small pig, here,' he said as his torch lit up Denzel's smiling face, 'and it couldn't have been HIM you were all scared of could it?'

Mucus glared at Denzel, and then he noticed that the sergeant had started to wander off towards the castle.

'You come back here, Hengist! Don't you DARE ignore me, or I'll tell Mummy!' he shouted furiously.

But the sergeant wasn't listening. He was whispering to himself.

'. . . and I was SO looking forward to going to Rome, with all the sunshine and the lovely food and everything. I had my holiday toga all packed and ready . . . and it wasn't SO much to ask, was it? Just one teensy weensy holiday?'

I began to see what Verucca meant. Even I was starting to feel sorry for the sergeant.

MUCUS (Totally furious)

Chapter Eleven

DRAGONS, WILD BOARS AND MAN-EATING BEARS

The next morning everyone was out inspecting the damage. Mucus and his friends had left an AWFUL mess and there were turnips and broken fences EVERYWHERE.

The grown-ups were all gathered under the Old Oak tree, drinking turnip tea and complaining.

'My nerves are in shreds!' wailed my mum. 'I haven't slept a wink ALL night.'

'I thought my hovel was going to fall down,' said Verucca's mum, Mildred.

'My hovel DID fall down, once!' said Urk's mum.

'Ooh, I remember that,' said Mildred. 'Wasn't that the time all them DRAGONS came rampaging through the village?'

'They weren't dragons – they was WILD BOARS,' said Eg's mum.

'Were they?' said Urk's mum. 'I could have sworn they were dragons, on account of their breathing fire and everything.'

'I don't remember any fire–breathing, but I DO remember when that great big bear ate your cousin. Does anybody want another cup of turnip tea?' said Mildred.

While the grown–ups carried on moaning, Burp and Vlad discovered that the posh boys had made a big hole in the pigsty wall, and some of the sick animals had got out.

'Little Hoppy the rabbit's escaped!' said Vlad, sniffing and dabbing at his eyes with a big dirty rag.

'He could be anywhere by now – all lost and frightened!'

'Horace the hedgehog AND Mabel the grass snake have gone too!' said Burp angrily. 'Horace has only got three legs, so he can't run very fast and Mabel's got NO sense of direction, so she won't know WHERE she is! Good thing I kept little Ron in my pocket.'

'Who's Ron?' I said.

'Ron's my rat, of COURSE, Sedric,' said Burp. 'The one your mum bashed with her broom.'

'Oh. THAT little Ron,' I said. I didn't like to ask how you could tell whether a snake had a sense of direction or not. Vlad and Burp were SO upset, so I said we'd all help them look for Horace, Mabel and Hoppy, and made a mental note to ask Gaius about the snake thing.

'Right,' I said. 'So we're looking for a three-legged hedgehog, a rabbit . . .'

'Oops. Nearly forgot to say. Hoppy's only got one ear,' said Vlad.

'OK. A three-legged hedgehog, a rabbit with one ear and a snake that's probably going round and round in circles,' I said, trying not to smile.

'It's not funny, Sedric,' said Burp. 'We HAVE to find them or they'll DIE!'

It was QUITE funny, but when great big tears welled up in his eyes and sploshed on to the mud, I felt a bit guilty.

'We WILL find them, Burp, I promise,' I said solemnly.

So we all split up and went off in different directions to look for a one-eared rabbit, a three-legged hedgehog and a confused snake. Verucca, Denzel and I started searching round the Old Oak Tree, where the grown-ups were all still moaning happily and drinking turnip tea.

'It was DEFINITELY them posh boys did all this damage, so we should tell the baron. He should do something about it,' said Eg's mum.

'You're quite right, of course, but the baron and his wife have gone on holiday,' said Gaius, who had joined in, but looked as if he wished he hadn't.

'Maybe we should have a word with Sergeant Hengist?'

'What's he got to do with it?' said Mildred. 'Who wants another cup of turnip tea?'

'WHAT HAPPENED TO THEM FLAPJACKS EVERYONE WAS GOING ON ABOUT?' shouted Eg's grandad.

'IT WAS RAT TRAPS, NOT FLAPJACKS, DAD!' shouted Eg's mum.

'What's a holiday?' said Urk's mum.

'Oh dear,' said Gaius.

Chapter Twelve

PiRATES, POSTS AND PARTiES

We didn't find Hoppy, Horace or Mabel near the Old Oak tree.

'They could be ANYWHERE,' said Eg grumpily, 'which means we could actually be looking for EVER.'

Which was true, so we were just deciding what to do next when we heard someone shouting.

'AHOY THERE! COULD YOU POSSIBLY DIRECT US TO THE CASTLE, IF IT'S NOT TOO MUCH TROUBLE?'

From out of the trees came a colourfully dressed man with a long silky yellow beard, standing on the front of the STRANGEST thing I had ever seen.

YB

Big pirate sails

CAPTAIN YELLOWBEA
(Not a PIRATEY pira

Flying lad
(with totally
NO top on

Big fat tattooed pirate

Small tattooed pirate

WHEELS (Not usually found on ~~boats~~ ship

It wasn't a boat and it wasn't a cart. It was a boat ON a cart, with huge sails and a flying lady on its front with totally NO top on.

She wasn't a REAL flying lady, obviously. That would have been weird. She was all carved from wood and painted in bright colours, and it was AWESOME. Urk nudged me and sniggered.

'She's got no top on,' he said.

'You are SO childish,' hissed Verucca.

Urk always sniggers at things like that. The word 'bum' makes him snigger too.

'Allow me to introduce myself,' said the colourfully dressed man. He took off his hat and bowed low. 'I am Captain Yellowbeard and I am a pirate, and this,' he added, waving his arm, 'is my motley crew.'

A group of tattooed pirates popped their heads out from the back of the boat/cart thing, and waved a cheery hello to us.

'Pleased to meet you too, Captain – er – Yellowbeard,' I said. 'I'm Sedric, and these are my friends. The castle's quite near actually – it's just up . . .'

'We learned about pirates in school,' Verucca interrupted suddenly. 'Our teacher told us that they're bloodthirsty and ruthless and they steal stuff.'

'Ah,' said Captain Yellowbeard, stroking his yellow beard. His voice was so smooth you could have spread it on a slice of bread. 'A common mistake. Your teacher must have been talking about a completely DIFFERENT sort of pirate. I'm the nice FRIENDLY sort, you see – not at all BAD, in fact. My first mate Hobnob here can tell you how lovely I am – can't you, Hobnob?'

A pirate with a wooden leg, a wooden crutch, a wooden arm and a wooden patch over one eye came stomping along the deck. He was pretty much made completely of wood.

HOBNOB

Wooden patch

Wooden grin

Wooden crutch

...oden arm →

Wooden leg

'You're lovely, Captain,' he said, grinning a wooden grin.

'There you are! So now you know how **VERY** lovely and nice I am, perhaps you could direct me to the castle? I have an invitation,' he said, pulling one of Mucus and Sinus's parchments out of his pocket.

'This leads me to believe that there is some sort of
revelry taking place this weekend, and as it's SUCH
bad form to be late . . .'

'I can show you the way, if you like,' said Rubella,
pushing past me. She was gazing admiringly at Captain
Yellowbeard's fancy clothes. 'Is this your boat? It's well
nice.'

'Hop aboard,' said Yellowbeard smoothly, 'but we pirates call them SHIPS, not BOATS.'

'I love your beard. Is it real?' said Rubella, reaching out to touch it.

'Don't touch the beard,' said Yellowbeard, jumping back. 'I mean it. NOBODY touches the beard.'

'Whatever. Can I bring my friend?' said Rubella.

'The more the merrier,' said Captain Yellowbeard, reaching down to help Gert aboard. 'We are going to a PARTY, after all!'

Chapter Thirteen

PIRATES, PLOTS AND TERRIBLE DANGERS

The pirate ship with Yellowbeard and his crew had just disappeared up the hill when Vlad and Burp came running out of the trees.

'Has a pirate with a yellow beard and a big boat come this way?' panted Vlad.

VLAD

BURP

'You just missed him,' I said. 'He's gone up to the castle. He seemed quite nice. He said he wasn't a PIRATEY sort of pirate.'

'WELL HE'S A GREAT BIG PIRATEY LIAR!' shouted Vlad.

'That's a bit harsh, Vlad!' I said. 'You haven't even met him.'

'Course I have,' he said angrily. 'He's my cousin, and he's a PROPER piratey pirate all right. Well – he used to be till he started suffering from seasickness REALLY bad, so he put wheels on his boat and he and his crew came ashore.'

'Ship,' said Eg. 'He said it was a ship.'

'But he seemed so NICE,' said Verucca.

'That's what he wanted you to think, but he's going to try and take over the castle! It's what he always does. Burp and me saw LOADS of his pirate gang swarming up the other side of the hill! He's up to no good, and if he does take over the castle, that means trouble for ALL OF US!'

'What do you mean?' I said.

'He's a REALLY nasty man,' said Vlad.

'But none of your family are very nice, Vlad. You told us that,' said Verucca.

'Well he's the WORST of them,' said Vlad darkly.

'What? Worse than your thieving, head–chopping dad?' I said.

'MUCH worse,' said Vlad.

Vlad's evil head-chopping dad

(and Yellowbeard is even WORSE than him.)

I was beginning to get a bit worried now.

'Blimey. What's he done?' asked Urk.

'You don't want to know. It'll give you nightmares,' said Vlad.

'HE'S TAKEN RUBELLA AND GERT!'

shouted Urk, running his hands frantically through his

stubbly hair and pinging nits off all over the place.

'GERT'S IN THE CLUTCHES OF AN EVIL PIRATE! WE HAVE TO RESCUE HER!'

Urk's monster nits pinging off.

He started to run up the hill after the ship/boat/
cart thing.

'Hold on, Urk!' said Verucca, grabbing hold of him.
'Stop! You can't rescue them on your own!'

'Verucca's right,' I said. 'We need to talk to Gaius.
He'll know what to do.'

So we found Gaius and told him everything.

'Yellowbeard'll have no problem taking over the
castle,' said Verucca. 'Roger and Norman told us that
the guards have totally stopped guarding things.
They're just getting drunk and playing cards all the
time.'

'Rubella and Gert are in TERRIBLE danger! We
have to SAVE them!' shouted Urk, running his hands
through his hair again and pinging off more nits.

We all moved away from him, and Robin pulled his
hood on tighter. Urk's nits are totally MONSTER.

'Well. If Rubella is stupid enough to get on a boat with a total stranger just because he's got a big beard and fancy clothes . . .' said Verucca.

'Ship,' said Eg. 'Yellowbeard said it was a **SHIP!**' **'WHATEVER!'** shouted Verucca.

Gaius looked very serious and thoughtful. 'If what you say is true, Vlad, then the whole village is in danger from this pirate cousin of yours. I believe we need to act fast to prevent Yellowbeard from carrying out his plans. You children must go up to the castle and keep watch, while I try to organise some support from the rest of the village. Don't do anything dangerous, and report back immediately if you see anything that . . .'

But we didn't hear the rest. We were already running up the hill.

Chapter Fourteen

IN WHICH YELLOWBEARD TAKES THE CASTLE
(QUITE EASILY ACTUALLY)

We saw the sails first.

The pirate ship was tied up outside the castle gates, but there was no sign of Yellowbeard OR his motley crew. The castle gates were wide open and there were no guards anywhere.

Then we heard some familiar annoying voices.

Mucus, Sinus and the other posh boys were all coming

over the top of the hill, heading for the castle doors.

'STOP!' I shouted, 'DON'T GO INTO THE CASTLE – IT'S NOT SAFE!'

'KEEP THAT PIG AWAY FROM ME! IT'S SAVAGE! IT ACTUALLY TRIED TO KILL ME!' shouted Mucus.

'WAIT, YOU NEED TO LISTEN TO US!' shouted Verucca. 'THERE ARE PIRATES IN THE CASTLE!'

'What are those peasants banging on about, Mucus?' said Sinus.

'Something about PIRATES!' said Mucus. 'Honestly, they really ARE stupid if they expect us to believe THAT! We're nowhere near the sea.'

'Just tell them that it's YOUR castle and to mind their own business,' said Sinus.

And before we could stop them, they all went

through the castle doors.

Then we heard an AWFUL lot of shouting. Mucus sounded especially cross. He kept yelling 'HENGIIIST!' and then it all went strangely quiet. The castle doors were still open and I didn't know what to do, so I quickly made a mental list and worked out there were four possibilities, which were:

1. Be really sensible and go straight back down to the village and tell Gaius what had happened.

OWW!

Eg worrying (he does this quite a LOT

94

2. Sit down and have a proper discussion about what to do next (highlighting possible dangers).

3. Storm the castle, shouting very loudly, but most probably be captured quite quickly and thrown in the dungeons.

4. Not do any of the above things.

So I did number 4, sort of, and shouted, 'WE SHOULD ALL GET INSIDE THE CASTLE WHILE THE DOORS ARE STILL OPEN!'

'But Gaius said not to do anything DANGEROUS!' said Eg anxiously. 'That is extremely and VERY dangerous.'

Eg was right of course, but then I

thought about what would happen if we **DIDN'T** get into the castle, and that was dangerous too, but in a different way.

So, in the end I stopped thinking and ran towards the castle doors, shouting, **'FOLLOW ME!'**

'OOWW!' shouted Urk, as he fell over a tussock. **'I THINK I'VE BROKEN MY LEG!'**

'AAGGH!' shouted Robin, as he fell over Urk.

'This is a seriously **NOT** a good idea, Sedric!' shouted Eg.

'I've got a stitch!' grunted Vlad. He didn't generally do running.

Denzel bounded through the castle doors, and Verucca and I followed him. We were only just in time, because Captain Yellowbeard roared,

US hiding (you can just see my legs)

'GOBBIT! PUTRID! LOCK THE DOORS
AND DON'T LET ANYONE IN!'

His silky–smooth voice wasn't quite so silky now.
We hid behind a load of barrels as two pirates strode
past us and slammed the doors shut.

'BULLWINKLE! YOU AND
DOGSBREATH TAKE THESE WHINY
LITTLE POSH BOYS DOWN TO THE
DUNGEONS AND THROW THEM IN
WITH THE OTHERS – THEY'RE
STARTING
TO
REALLY
GET ON
MY NERVES!'

Gobbit

Putrid

I began to warm to Yellowbeard a little bit when he said that. But then he shouted, 'THE CASTLE IS MINE!' and did a sort of mad cackly laugh, so I unwarmed to him again. I realised that Vlad was right – he was definitely a BAD man, and also most probably mad as well.

Yellowbeard doing mad CACKLY laugh →

The two pirates finished fastening all the bolts on the castle doors and sat down on the barrels.

'The Captain's well chuffed with how easy it all was,' said the small pirate. 'What sort of idiots go away and leave a WHOLE castle COMPLETELY undefended?'

'Have you seen the way they've decorated it though, Putrid?' said the big one. 'It's well nice. Fancy without being too in-your-face. I'm going to like living here.'

'Me too,' said Putrid. 'It's well comfy, and I love all them soft cushions everywhere.'

And while they were talking about Prunehilda's choice of soft furnishings, I reviewed our situation.

1. We – that is Verucca, Denzel and I – were **INSIDE** the locked and bolted castle doors, with an awful lot of probably mad pirates and their definitely mad captain, which wasn't good.

2. Everyone else was **OUTSIDE** the locked and bolted doors. That also wasn't good, because they couldn't get in.

Everyone **OUTSIDE** castle doors (seriously <u>not</u> good)

3, I had a cramp in one leg. And that was REALLY not good. You can't ignore cramp. It just gets worse and worse until you HAVE to wiggle your feet or jump up and down.

'I have to move now,' I whispered to Verucca. 'Good idea. Those pirates are WELL boring,' whispered a very small voice that wasn't Verucca's.

It was Burp.

Chapter Fifteen

LOTS OF HIDING IN STRANGE PLACES

(LIKE CUPBOARDS AND TOILETS)

'BURP! What are you DOING here?' hissed Verucca.

US - quite surprised at meeting Burp behind the barrels

'Sedric told us to get inside the castle, so I did,' Burp whispered back.

'I didn't mean YOU!' I hissed.

'Why not? What's wrong with me?' whispered Burp.

'Ssshh! Keep your voice down. We're not cross with you. Well, I am a bit, but it's just because I don't want you to get hurt,' whispered Verucca. 'It's going to be very dangerous.'

'Denzel's here,' Burp whispered. 'He could get hurt too.'

'Denzel's different,' I said. 'He hasn't got a mum who would go completely bonkers if anything happened to him, like you have.'

'Ron's here too,' he whispered. 'He's in my pocket.'

'Who's Ron?' whispered Verucca.

'He's the rat my mum hit with the broom,' I whispered.

'And we might find Hoppy, Mabel and Horace in here

too,' said Burp. 'After all, Eg did say they could be anywhere.'

Which was true, but I wasn't sure that was what Eg had meant.

'He did,' whispered Verucca. 'You can keep an eye out for them, but you need to stay close to me and keep REALLY quiet, OK?'

'OK,' whispered Burp happily.

Gobbit and Putrid didn't see us as we crept out from behind the barrels. They were too busy talking about Prunehilda's naked Roman statues, which they both agreed needed some clothes.

As we crept through the castle we saw that there was loads of food and rubbish all over the place, and the posh boys had broken quite a lot of stuff too.

'When Prunehilda sees what Mucus and his stupid friends have done she's going to go totally mental! WHAT ARE YOU DOING, SEDRIC?'

Verucca hissed as I suddenly stopped and pushed her
and Burp through a door.

'YUK! It's WELL stinky in here,' said Burp,
holding his nose.

BAD SMELL →

'I thought I heard someone coming, and I think we're
in the toilets,' I whispered.

'What are toilets?' whispered Burp.

'You don't want to know,' I said quietly. 'It's a Roman thing.

ROMAN TOILET

N.B* There's no bucket for chucking stuff out of window – SMELLY!

Roman toilet roll → (sponge on stick - YUK)

★ N.B : Nota bene - which is Latin for PAY ATTENTION.

'There's a BIG SPIDER in here!' said a loud familiar voice from inside a cupboard in the corner of the room. 'I don't like spiders. I hope they don't have big spiders in Rome.'

'Ssh, sarge. You're not going to Rome. We're in a

cupboard, and do you remember what we said about you just whispering?' said another familiar voice from inside the same cupboard.

'You're standing on my toga. They wear togas in Rome, did you know that?' said the sergeant loudly.

'Ssshh, sarge – remember, just little whispers!'

'Roger?' said Verucca, through the cupboard door.

'THERE'S NO ONE IN HERE! IT'S JUST AN EMPTY CUPBOARD!' said Roger's voice.

I opened the door.

'Oh, it's just YOU,' said Roger, looking relieved. 'How did you all get in here? Did Yellowbeard's pirates see you?'

'No, we managed to hide from them,' I said. 'What are you doing in here?'

'Well – it's quite a long story. Captain Yellowbeard and his crew arrived and said they'd come for the party,' said Norman. 'He was ever so friendly at first, but then he suddenly told his crew to throw us in the dungeons, because he was taking over the castle. Me and Rog managed to escape with the sarge here, and we've been hiding in this cupboard ever since, haven't we Rog?'

'We have, Norm,' said Roger. 'The sarge isn't himself though. He's taken the disappointment over losing his holiday very badly. It's made him go a bit . . .'

'Sshh! I can hear someone coming!' said Verucca.

'Get in here, quick!' said Norman, pulling us all inside the cupboard and shutting the door just in time.

US (a bit squashed) inside cupboard

We heard the door to the toilets open and then close again, and a gruff piratey voice said,

'. . . and then I got this tattoo of a skull and crossbones, with this cutlass and flower motif. What do you think, Gobbit? Tell me honestly now.'

'It's well lovely, Putrid. I'd like one like that. Where'd you get it done?' said Gobbit.

'That bloke down the tavern done it,' said Putrid. 'It went a bit scabby and 'orrible at first but it's healed up lovely now. I specially like the colours he's done the flowers.'

'Careful, Sedric. You're squashing Ron,' whispered Burp from the corner of the cupboard.

'Sorry,' I whispered back.

'What are we going to do about these pirates?' whispered Verucca.

'Pirates? I know a song about pirates. Do you want me to sing it?' whispered Sergeant Hengist. 'I can see them through this little tiny crack.'

'No!' whispered Roger frantically. 'No shouting OR singing, sarge!'

'I think we should just stay in here and keep quiet and maybe they'll go away. It worked last time, didn't it, Rog?' whispered Norman.

'But shouldn't we DO something, like bash them on the head?' said Verucca. 'There's a broom in here. You could use that.'

'What - US? Bash them on the head?' whispered Roger, sounding horrified.

'You ARE soldiers,' I whispered. 'You must have had training or something?'

'Well,' whispered Roger. 'Some of the others went on a course a while back, but Norm had a cold so he couldn't go, and I . . .'

'Oh, for goodness' sake!' Verucca said, grabbing the broom and bursting out of the doors. The two pirates

were very surprised to see her. They were very
surprised to see ALL of us actually, and while
they were being surprised, Verucca quickly
bopped them both on the head with the
broom. Roger and Norman tied them up,
and then we looked around for
somewhere to hide them.

The cupboard was the only
place big enough, but we had to
persuade Sergeant Hengist to
come out first. He said he didn't
want to come out because he

Verucca head bopping

liked it in the cupboard, and if he had to come out he
might see the horrible boys who had spoiled his holiday
and then he'd get all depressed and angry again, and
he didn't want to get depressed and angry, and he
made so much noise that another pirate came in to
see what was going on, so Verucca had to bop that
pirate on the head too. Then two more arrived so she
bopped them as well, and by the time Roger and Norman
had tied them up, the cupboard was totally full of
unconscious pirates.

Pile of PIRATES

'Well, this is all going VERY well,' said Roger happily. 'I reckon it won't be long until we've tied up ALL the pirates, and then we can let the guards out of the dungeons and get the castle back.'

'That sounds simple,' I said, 'but we can't just wait in the toilets for pirates to bop on the head. The cupboard's full up, so we've got nowhere else to hide them, and if any more came in they might notice their friends lying all over the floor.'

'Hadn't thought of that, had we Rog?' said Norman.

'No,' said Roger. 'So, what are we going to do next then?'

It was quite difficult creeping round the castle without being seen. Denzel kept running off and sniffing things, and Sergeant Hengist kept shouting and wanting to sing his pirate song. Roger had to tell him he wasn't allowed to shout OR sing.

'Can I shout if I see a pirate?' he whispered.

'No, sarge. You must DEFINITELY not do that,' said Roger.

'What about if there's a troll that's going to eat us – or a dragon? Can I shout if I see a dragon?'

'No shouting, sarge. Not even if you see a dragon,' whispered Norman.

'Do you really think we can rescue Rubella and Gert AND get the castle back before someone finds us and throws us in the dungeons?' whispered Verucca.

'Don't see why not,' whispered Roger cheerfully. 'We just need to keep bopping the pirates on the head and hiding them in cupboards until they're all gone.'

'But we don't know how many pirates there really are,' I said. 'There were only a few on Captain Yellowbeard's boat.'

'Me and Vlad saw LOADS of them!' whispered Burp.'

'And what's all this WE stuff, anyway?' whispered Verucca. 'I'm the only one bopping the pirates on the head!'

'Yeah, but we're excellent at tying them up, aren't we, Rog?' said Norman. 'That's a special skill that is – tying things up.'

'I got a badge for tying things, haven't I Norm?' said Roger proudly.

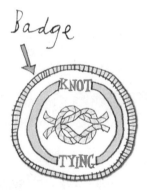

Badge

KNOT TYING

We reached the Great Hall, which was very scary owing to the raucous pirate voices and loud singing that reached us through the thick wooden doors.

'Sounds like there are quite a lot of pirates in there,' whispered Roger.

Suddenly the doors opened and a few of the pirates came out. We all ducked behind a big curtain before they saw us, and for a tiny second we could see inside the Great Hall.

There were an AWFUL lot of pirates in there.

Chapter Sixteen

AN AWFUL LOT OF PiRATES
(THERE REALLY WERE TOTALLY LOADS!)

It was a bit of a squash behind the curtain, but there
was nowhere else to hide.

Denzel (wriggly and annoying)   Verucca getting cross

Sergeant Hengist had finally stopped shouting but kept saying 'SSHHHH!' very loudly. I had to hold on tightly to Denzel who was getting bored and wriggly.

'Right,' I whispered. 'Has anybody got any ideas?'

'We could look for Hoppy, Horace and Mabel,' whispered Burp.

'Maybe now isn't exactly the right time, Burp,' said Verucca. 'Any OTHER ideas?'

'Ideas about what?' said Roger.

'About getting rid of Yellowbeard and getting the castle back, of course!' said Verucca.

'Oh, that. Well . . .' he said slowly, 'we could er – maybe – um . . .'

We waited.

'Anything?' I said.

'No,' he said finally. 'My mind's a blank. Norm?'

'What?' asked Norman.

'You got any ideas?'

'Well,' said Norman, even more slowly. 'The head—bopping thing has worked quite well so far, so I'm thinking . . .'

'Have you SEEN how many pirates are in there? I can't possibly bop them ALL on the head!' hissed Verucca angrily. 'Maybe you should have gone on that training course, then you wouldn't be quite so USELESS!'

Which I thought was a BIT unkind, but I didn't say anything.

'If we could just see inside the Great Hall, we might be able to make some sort of a plan,' I said.

'There's a little slitty window up there, Sedric,' whispered Burp, pointing above my head. 'You could look through that.'

Little high up pointy window →

'Brilliant idea, Burp!' I said. 'Except it's a bit high up.'

'You could stand on our shoulders,' said Norman.

'Brilliant idea, Norm!' I said.

'Not so useless now, am I?' said Norman, looking at Verucca.

So Verucca and I climbed up on to Roger and Norman's shoulders and peeped through the little slitty window. The Great Hall was totally FULL of pirates, and in the middle of it was Rubella, shouting at Captain Yellowbeard, which I didn't think was a VERY good idea after Vlad telling us how seriously BAD and MEAN he was.

'I thought you WANTED my opinion!' Rubella shouted. 'All I said was that shade of purple doesn't go with red!'

'I'M BORED NOW!' shouted Captain Yellowbeard. 'BORED, BORED, BORED! In fact I'm SO bored I think I'll make you and your funny little friend walk the plank, then maybe you'll think twice about being RUDE about people's clothes!!'

'You shouldn't ask for somebody's style advice if you don't want to hear the truth, and talking about the TRUTH, you lied about wanting to come to Mucus's party, AND you're not a REAL pirate anyway because you haven't even got a proper BOAT!' shouted Rubella.

'IT'S A SHIP!' shouted Yellowbeard. 'What part of "IT'S A SHIP" don't you get? Take them away, Bullwinkle!'

'Yes, Captain! Straight away, Captain! Shall I get the new plank out now?' said Bullwinkle excitedly as he dragged Rubella and Gert away.

'What an excellent idea, Bullwinkle,' said Yellowbeard.

Rubella and Gert dragged off by PIRATE →

'Dogsbreath! Bring me that whiny boy with the enormous teeth who claims he's the baron's son!'

A small wiry pirate appeared, pushing Mucus through the crowd.

'Right,' growled Yellowbeard, leaning forward so his face was right up close to Mucus's. 'I want you to tell me where **DADDY** keeps all his gold, and if you don't, I'll have to ask Dogsbreath here to er – **PERSUADE** you!'

Dogsbreath grinned a toothless grin. Mucus went white.

'W - W - WHEN MY FATHER GETS BACK HE'LL HAVE YOU ARRESTED AND THROWN IN THE DUNGEONS AND - AND - THEN HE'LL HAVE YOU TORTURED WITH HOT SPIKY THINGS! HE CAN YOU KNOW!' squawked Mucus.

I have to admit I was quite impressed. Either Mucus was being brave or he was more stupid than I thought and he REALLY didn't have any idea how incredibly mad and nasty Yellowbeard was.

'WHEN is your father going to do all this? When he's overpowered ALL my motley crew and released ALL his guards from the dungeons? I DON'T think so!' Yellowbeard leaned back in Dennis's chair. 'This is MY castle now, and I'M in charge! Now, talking of having HORRIBLE THINGS done to you, it would be SO much less painful for BOTH of us if you would just tell me where Daddy keeps his cash!'

Dennis's CASH

'I don't know where he keeps it and even if I did I wouldn't tell YOU!' shouted Mucus.

'Take him back down to the dungeons!' shouted Yellowbeard. 'A bit longer with the RATS might jog his memory!'

Mucus looking WELL scared

'GOT THE PLANK READY, CAPTAIN!' shouted Bullwinkle.

Yellowbeard swaggered over and squinted at it.

'Are you sure you've put it together right?' he said.

'Think so, Captain,' said Bullwinkle. 'Here's the manual. It says, "Congratulations for choosing the

Superplank Series 4. The new features will give you hours of . . .'"

Bullwinkle and instructions
for PLANK ↗

'You idiot! You've put it together upside down!' interrupted Yellowbeard, snatching the parchment from Bullwinkle's hands.

'Sorry, Captain,' said Bullwinkle. 'I'll have it right in a jiffy.'

'Sedric, we're going to have to do something fast,' whispered Verucca. 'This plank thing sounds REALLY – you know – final.'

Then, from below us, Roger sneezed. Verucca wobbled, slid down the wall and landed on Sergeant Hengist, who'd been having a little nap underneath.

'AAGGHH! What's happening! Where am I? Is the ship sinking? Is this Rome?' shouted the sergeant.

'Ssh, sarge,' whispered Norman. 'You're not IN Rome. You're still in the castle.'

'Who's in there?' came a gruff piratey voice from the other side of the curtain.

'RUN!' shouted Verucca, pulling back the curtain and giving a wild swing with her broom. The pirate grunted and fell to the floor and we all ran as fast as we could back the way we'd come.

PIRATE
(head bopped by Verucca's broom)

We reached the door leading to the kitchens, so I signalled to the others and we all pounded down the stairs.

I was praying that we wouldn't find any pirates waiting at the bottom.

Chapter Seventeen

MEN IN FROCKS

'You're not getting any more food till you all learns some manners, so you might as well turn around and get back up them stairs!' shouted a big scary woman who stood at the bottom of the stairs.

'We're not pirates!' I panted. 'We've actually just escaped from them and –'

← Big scary woman

'Oooh, Sergeant Hengist?!' she said, interrupting me and changing her tone. 'Are you all right, deary? You don't look yourself.'

'He's not been well,' said Roger. 'It's all been too much for him.'

'You poor love! You look like you need a great big hug. Come here,' she said, grabbing hold of the sergeant and giving him a squeeze that went on a little bit too long. 'You need to get rid of them pirates,' she said to Roger and Norman.

'They got NO manners at all, AND they got appetites like pigs!' she added.

Then she spotted Denzel. 'I could do something with him,' she said. 'I've got a recipe for a lovely boiled pork with apple sauce and spices . . .'

But before I could explain that Denzel wasn't there to be cooked, Hobnob the pirate came clunking woodenly down the stairs.

Roger and Norman quickly pulled Sergeant Hengist out of sight, while Verucca and I tried to look like we worked in the kitchens and were looking for something in a barrel.

'The Captain says he's hungry!' announced Hobnob.

'The Captain says he's hungry WHAT?' shouted the cook angrily.

'He's just sort of . . . hungry,' said Hobnob, looking confused.

'You tell your Captain that til he learns his pleases

and thank yous he's not getting **NOTHIN'** more from me!' she snapped.

'She's only joking,' said Verucca suddenly, stepping in front of Hobnob and curtseying. 'Such a joker, aren't you . . . er, er . . .'

'Gladys,' said the cook.

'Right. Gladys. She's always kidding around! Tell the Captain we'll be up with something tasty in a jiffy.'

Verucca and me looking in barrel (using **STEALTH**)

'Righty ho,' said Hobnob, clumping woodenly back up the stairs.

'DON'T BOTHER SAYIN' THANK YOU!' shouted Gladys, as we all stared at Verucca. Had she gone completely bonkers?

It turned out she hadn't – but she did have a plan that was a bit bonkers. Well, it wasn't even exactly a plan. It was more of a vague idea. She said that to rescue Gert and Rubella, we had to get into the Great Hall as quickly as possible without being noticed and the best way we could do that was to disguise ourselves as maids.

'You'll have to 'cos none of us is goin' up there waiting on them ill-mannered yobs,' said a sulky looking maid who was sitting next to the fire. 'We told 'em we're not doin' NOTHIN'! We're on strike!'

Sulky maid ➤

'But even if you DO get into the Great Hall,' said Roger, 'what can you two do on your own?'

'But it won't just be me and Sedric,' said Verucca. 'You, Norm and the sergeant are going to dress as maids too!'

'Don't be daft,' said Roger. 'We're not GIRLS!'

'Have you got any spare dresses down here?' Verucca asked Gladys, ignoring Roger. 'We might need an extra big one for the sergeant.'

'You can't send the sergeant up with all them pirates – not in the state he's in! You leave him down here with me,' said Gladys, moving in to give Sergeant Hengist another great big squeeze.

'Thank you very much, but I'll go with them if that's all right,' said the sergeant, nervously backing away.

'Remember, sarge. You have to pretend you're a maid. You'll need to curtsey and talk in a high voice,' said Roger.

'And you definitely CAN'T sing your pirate song,' said Verucca. 'Are you sure you can manage it?'

'I can. Just don't leave me with HER,' he whispered, nervously.

So we all wriggled into our maids' dresses. Sergeant Hengist looked a bit weird, but less weird than he'd looked in the toga, and Roger's and Norman's chins were a bit stubbly, but Verucca said that if they kept their heads down no one would notice.

'You look lovely, sarge,' said Norman kindly. 'That shade of blue goes nicely with your beard.'

'We might be in disguise, but we still don't know what we're actually going to do when we get INSIDE the Great Hall,' I said. 'How are we going to rescue Rubella and Gert without the pirates stopping us?'

'We need to put them out of action somehow,' said Verucca.

'But HOW?' said Roger.

'We could POISON them,' said Norman.

'Killing people is WRONG, Norm,' said Roger.

'Yeah, I know,' said Norman slowly, 'but making people SICK isn't.'

'That is a BRILLIANT idea, Norm,' I said.

Norman was SO pleased that he'd come up with another brilliant idea. We worked out we could poison the pirates just enough so that they'd be sick and not able to do mean and piratey things, but not enough to actually kill them. And while they were being sick, WE could rescue Rubella and Gert and let the guards out of the dungeons. We searched the kitchen and found some chicken legs that Gladys said she'd cooked days ago, and the sulky maid pointed to where some flies were buzzing round and said, 'there's some well rank stuff in them bins over there, if you REALLY

BIN →
(with rats and flies)

want to poison them pirates. There's **RATS** in there, too,' she added.

'How's Little Ron, Burp?' I said, suddenly remembering.

Burp gently lifted the tiny limp rat out of his pocket and peered at him. 'I think he's a bit better, Sedric,' he said

'That's brilliant,' Verucca said.

'Yes,' said Burp, smiling happily. 'But there's loads of rat poo in my pocket now.'

'Oh dear,' said Verucca. 'We can get Mum to clean it out later.'

'Wait, isn't rat poo really **UNHYGIENIC**?'

asked Norman slowly. 'Couldn't it make you SICK?'

'You are a GENIUS, Norman!' said Verucca.

Norman smiled happily and blushed at his Good Idea Number 3.

Norman feeling WELL pleased due to Good idea No.3

So we mixed rat poo and some mouldy stuff from the bins into some gravy and poured it over the chicken legs. Gladys arranged them on plates and decorated them with leaves and slices of apple to make them look more tasty.

'That smells delicious,' said Roger. 'I'd eat some if I didn't know it'd make me puke.'

'Burp, you and Ron need to stay down here with Gladys,' said Verucca. 'It might get a bit dangerous and I don't want you to get hurt.'

'They'll be fine with me,' said Gladys. 'Now, just remember to curtsey a lot – and keep your heads down!'

'Righty ho,' I said, as Verucca, Roger, Norman and Sergeant Hengist and I carefully carried the plates up the stairs to the Great Hall.

Dodgy chicken

I took Denzel with me. I didn't think it was a good idea to leave him in the kitchens. I didn't like the way Gladys was looking at him.

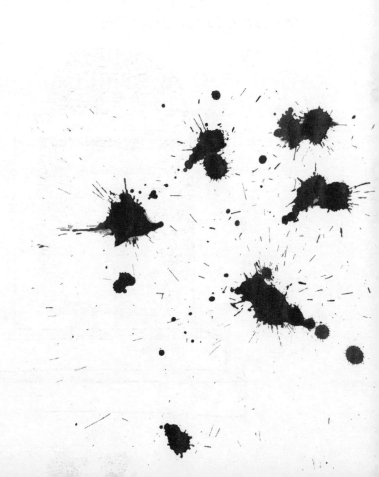

Chapter Eighteen

PIRATE PUKE AND PLANKWALKING

'THE FOOD'S HERE, CAPTAIN!' shouted
Bullwinkle, as we arrived in the Great Hall.

Great big dirty pirate hands grabbed at the meat
as I pushed my way through, curtseying and smiling.

Dirty pirate hands

'That smells lovely,' growled a big pirate with a whole ship tattooed on his cheek. Norman curtseyed to all the pirates, saying, 'Chicken leg, sir?' in a high voice. He was VERY good.

The food was disappearing fast, so Verucca and I tried to edge our way over to where Rubella and Gert were standing tied together on the Superplank Series 4. The end they were standing on was balanced on a table,

Superplank Series 4

while the other stuck out of a window, with a VERY long drop down to the hard ground below.

Vlad was right. Yellowbeard really was a VERY bad man.

'YOU CAN START WALKING THE PLANK AS SOON AS I'VE FINISHED THIS DELICIOUS CHICKEN LEG!' shouted Yellowbeard. 'DON'T START WITHOUT ME!'

'We need to get to Rubella and Gert NOW!' I whispered to Verucca.

Suddenly a pirate pushed past us with his hand over his mouth.

'Don't feel well!' he mumbled.

Pirate about to throw up

Then, all over the Great Hall, pirates were starting to groan, and gradually the groaning got louder and louder as the mouldy chicken and rat poo began to work, and the throwing-up noises began.

← MORE pirates about to throw up

We edged nearer and nearer to Rubella and Gert, and had just reached them when Captain Yellowbeard's voice suddenly cut through the horrible noises.

'THERE'S SOMETHING VERY

ODD GOING ON HERE! WHY IS EVERYONE BEING SICK AND WHY DOES THAT MAID HAVE A BEARD?'

he shouted, pointing at the sergeant.

'It's not her fault, Captain,' squeaked Norman. 'Her mum's got one too. She's a bit self-conscious about it, so we never mention it.'

'That's right,' growled the sergeant. 'I'm a girl – really I am.'

'IF THAT'S A GIRL, THEN I'M THE EMPEROR OF ROME!

Yellowbeard spottin
Sergeant Hengist
← BEARD

ARREST THOSE MAIDS!' yelled Yellowbeard,
'AND YOU TWO ON THE PLANK!
START WALKING!'

'Jump!' shouted Verucca.

Rubella and Gert jumped down off the plank and we quickly untied them.

'NOW RUN!' I shouted.

So we did.

Verucca, Denzel, Rubella and Gert, Roger, Norman, Sergeant Hengist and I ran and ran across the Great Hall, through all the pirates and the pirate sick, towards the doors.

'STOP THEM!' shouted Captain Yellowbeard.

'Is he REALLY the Emperor of Rome?' panted Roger.

'This is SO gross!' said Rubella. 'Why is everyone throwing up?'

'Just stop complaining and run,' said Verucca. 'We have actually just rescued you from certain death, in case you hadn't noticed!'

'PULL YOURSELVES TOGETHER, YOU USELESS IDIOTS AND CATCH THEM BEFORE THEY GET AWAY!'

shouted Captain Yellowbeard to the groaning, puking pirates, 'AND WILL SOMEONE GET THIS BLASTED PIG OUT OF THE WAY BEFORE I BREAK MY NECK!'

We finally reached the doors and burst through into the corridor and I was just giving Denzel a silent cheer for doing his trying-to-trip-people-up thing, when I tripped over my skirt, slid along the floor and crashed into a wall.

I looked up.

ME (in a BIT of a pickle)

Yellowbeard was standing over me. He was all alone. His motley crew were far behind, still groaning and throwing up.

'GOT YOU, YOU INTERFERING LITTLE PEASANT!' he shouted.

'NO YOU HAVEN'T! YOU'RE ON YOUR OWN NOW, YELLOWBEARD!'

I shouted as loudly and dramatically as I could, so Verucca and the others could hear me. **'SO YOU MIGHT AS WELL GIVE YOURSELF UP!'**

The others stopped running and turned around.

'NEVER! THIS IS MY CASTLE NOW!' shouted Yellowbeard, looking around desperately for help. He spotted Gert, who wasn't very good at running and was puffing along, trying to keep up with the others, and he grabbed hold of her.

Gert a bit puffed

'IF ANYONE TRIES TO STOP ME – YOUR LITTLE FUNNY LITTLE FRIEND GETS IT!' he yelled.

'BITE HIM, GERT!' yelled Rubella.

Gert bit down hard on Captain Yellowbeard's hand. Yellowbeard yelled and dropped her, and at that very same moment, a door flew open behind him and knocked him flat on his face.

Urk's nits flying off (well not really flying. They don't have any wings.)

Through the door burst Urk, Robin, Eg, and Vlad and they trampled over the flattened body of Captain Yellowbeard.

'SHE'S NOT FUNNY! SHE'S LOVELY!' shouted Urk, going red.

'URRGGHHHHHHHHH!!' said Yellowbeard.

Then the door burst open a second time and the castle guards came bursting through, and trampled all over Captain Yellowbeard AGAIN.

'AARRGGHHHHH!' groaned Yellowbeard again, trying to get up, but the door burst open for a third time and the posh boys burst through, braying and snorting and trampled on him AGAIN.

'What's happening? Bullwinkle? Hobnob?' Yellowbeard groaned weakly and passed out.

'But how on earth did you all get in?' I said, after we'd hugged and jumped up and down a bit. 'The

URRGGHH!

pirates locked all the doors.'

'They locked the BIG doors but they didn't know about the tiny nipping-in-and-out door into the dungeons that we used to rescue Denzel, when the baron kidnapped him that time,' said Robin. 'We got into the dungeons through that, let the guards and the posh boys out and here we are!'

I was about to tell them all about OUR adventures and hiding in the toilets and Sergeant Hengist thinking he was in Rome and the head—bopping and poisoning

Yellowbeard and the pirates, when we heard someone

hammering on the castle doors. A voice shouted,

'WHERE IN HADES IS EVERYONE?
WILL SOMEBODY OPEN THIS
BLASTED DOOR AND LET US IN?'

It sounded horribly like the baron.

Chapter Nineteen

IN WHICH DENNIS IS DEFINITELY NOT A HAPPY BUNNY

Roger and Norman ran to open the doors, which took a while owing to Gobbit and Putrid having fastened totally ALL the bolts.

'WON'T BE A MINUTE, SIRE!' shouted Roger. 'I'm all fingers and thumbs, Norm. Why do you suppose the baron's come back?'

'Don't know, Rog. P'raps he got homesick, or seasick or something. NEARLY THERE, SIRE - ONLY A COUPLE MORE BOLTS TO GO!' shouted Norman, as the baron shouted a lot of angry rude words from the other side of the doors.

'There you are, sire!' said Roger, opening the doors and letting a furious and dishevelled baron and an even more furious and dishevelled Prunehilda push past him, followed by Boris and Lucretia, who looked pretty furious and dishevelled too.

Furious and dishevelled (which means a bit of a mess)

'It's lovely to have you back, sire,' said Norman.

'Did you enjoy your holiday?'

'DO WE LOOK LIKE WE ENJOYED OUR HOLIDAY, YOU IDIOT? OF COURSE WE DIDN'T ENJOY OUR HOLIDAY. AND DO YOU WANT TO KNOW WHY WE DIDN'T ENJOY OUR HOLIDAY? WELL I'LL TELL YOU. IT'S BECAUSE WE HAVEN'T ACTUALLY HAD A HOLIDAY! WE DIDN'T EVEN GET HALFWAY TO ROME, THANKS TO SOME PESKY PIRATES WHO ATTACKED US WHEN WE'D BARELY SET SAIL AND STOLE EVERYTHING! WE HAD TO BEG RIDES IN FILTHY CARTS FROM COMMON PEASANTS - AND WE EVEN

HAD TO - TO - WALK SOME
OF THE WAY, JUST TO GET
HOME!'

'The indignity of it all . . .' groaned Prunehilda
as they all staggered past us and into the castle.
'I'll NEVER get over it, and I am NEVER
going to go on holiday again!'

'I've never been so insulted in ALL my life!'
gasped Lucretia. 'Imagine having to share a cart
with three peasants AND a pig! The SMELL was
AWFUL!'

'It's going to give me nightmares for months.
HENGIST! RUN ME A HOT BATH!'
squawked Prunehilda. 'It's such a relief to be back in
my lovely clean castle, with all my lovely . . .'

But then she glanced down and saw the mess and
the broken statues and the curtains and food all over
the floor.

'AAARRRGGHH!
DENNIS! WHAT
IN THE WHOLE
OF HADES HAS
BEEN GOING
ON HERE?!
TELL ME IT'S
NOT REALLY HAPPENING! TELL ME
IT'S A HIDEOUS NIGHTMARE! MY
BEAUTIFUL CASTLE IS RUINED!'
she screamed, staring at the mess in horror.

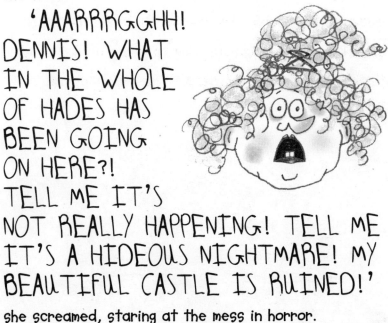

'Where is Hengist?' growled the baron, **'I DEMAND AN EXPLANATION!'**

'He's here, sire,' said Roger, 'but I think I need to explain, sire. He's not been quite himself since you left. The disappointment hit him hard. He'd been so looking forward to his holiday, and then when . . .'

Dennis was staring at Roger, Norman and the sergeant in disbelief, like he'd only just noticed them. **'WHY ARE YOU IDIOTS WEARING DRESSES?'** he bellowed.

'It's a bit complicated, isn't it, Norm?' said Roger.

'Good grief! Don't tell me!' said Dennis, and he turned to the sergeant. 'HENGIST! I HOLD YOU ENTIRELY RESPONSIBLE FOR ALL THIS . . . THIS . . . !' Dennis shouted, waving his arms around as he tried to find a suitable word.

'I – er . . . Well, you see, sire . . .' said the sergeant weakly.

'Well, WHAT? SPEAK UP MAN!' shouted Dennis furiously.

I thought it was REALLY unfair to blame the sergeant, so I stepped forward.

'Excuse me, sire,' I said.

'What in Hades are YOU doing here?' roared Dennis.

'It's a long story, but none of this is the sergeant's fault, sire,' I said.

ME weirdly ∧ sticking up for Sergeant Hengist

'He's done his best, but what with the pirates turning up and everything . . .'

'PIRATES?! PIRATES!? What do you mean PIRATES?' spluttered Dennis.

'It was Captain Yellowbeard and his motley crew . . .' I said. 'They told us . . .'

'Do you mean to tell me that PIRATES have been here, in MY castle?' gasped Dennis.

'They're actually still here, sire,' said Roger. 'They've been a bit sick in the Great Hall, so you might want to watch where you put your feet.'

Pirate puke

'They told us that they'd come for the PARTY, but they were lying and they took over the castle instead.' I was determined to get to the end of the story, even though Dennis KEPT ON interrupting me.

'PARTY?' shouted Dennis. 'WHAT PARTY? DO YOU KNOW ABOUT

THIS, HENGIST?'

'Well, sire, it – it was um – young – er . . .' the sergeant was looking confused.

'STOP BLATHERING, MAN! WHAT IN HADES IS WRONG WITH YOU?' yelled Dennis, which just made the sergeant even MORE confused, so I carried on.

'It was Mucus's party. He and Sinus sent out loads of invitations, and Yellowbeard found one and . . .'

'MUCUS!' bellowed Dennis.

MUCUUUS!

Chapter Twenty

PEASANTS, PiGS AND WHOPPiNG GREAT LIES

The pale and dishevelled figure of Mucus pushed through the posh boys and staggered towards Prunehilda, who screamed, 'MY BABYKINS! WHAT HAVE THEY DONE TO YOU?'

But as Mucus went towards her, arms outstretched, he suddenly spotted Rubella. His mouth dropped open and his eyes went all goggly (in manner of frightened rabbit and hungry

← Mucus - acting like frightened rabbit etc. again.

fox etc. etc. again) and he missed Prunehilda's arms
and fell into Rubella's instead.

    'GET YOUR HORRIBLE PEASANT
HANDS OFF MY BABYKINS!' screamed
Prunehilda, launching herself at a very surprised
Rubella and trying to wrench Mucus's arms from around
her neck.

Prunehilda really ← VERY angry

'OH MUCUS! Get away from HER! you must be in SHOCK after your awful ordeal - you don't know what you're doing! She's nothing but a - a - a - dirty COMMON PEASANT!'

'WHO ARE YOU CALLING DIRTY AND COMMON, YOU OLD BAG?' shouted Rubella.

'DENNIS! DID YOU HEAR WHAT SHE CALLED ME? Ooooh! I can feel one of my turns coming on!' wailed Prunehilda, clutching at her throat where her jewellery used to be.

'MUCUS!' growled Dennis. 'I want a word with you!'

'Oh, Hades! What's happening? Who is this peasant and where am I?' cried Mucus weakly, recoiling from Rubella with a horrified look on his face. 'It's all been simply HIDEOUS since you and Mumsy left, Daddy. These horrible peasants have wrecked the castle, and they let the pirates in, and Hengist didn't do ANYTHING to stop them!'

'THAT IS SUCH A LIE!' shouted Rubella. 'SHUT THAT PEASANT UP AND TAKE THE REST OF THEM DOWN TO THE DUNGEONS!' roared Dennis. 'AND ARREST THE PIG, TOO! Send it down to Gladys in the kitchens. See if she can do that yummy pork thing with apple sauce and spices!'

But before the guards could make a move towards us, I spotted something yellow out of the corner of my eye. It was moving unsteadily towards the castle doors.

'IT'S YELLOWBEARD! STOP HIM –

HE'S GETTING AWAY!' I shouted.

And while the guards were making up their minds whether to arrest us or go after Yellowbeard, Denzel raced towards the escaping pirate and ducked between his legs. Yellowbeard wobbled a bit, Denzel doubled back and tripped him again, and then there was a thump and Yellowbeard crumpled to the ground.

A moment later, Gaius's smiling face appeared round the castle doors. He was holding Urk's Sticket bat.

'I do hope I didn't hit him too hard,' he said mildly.

'But I thought I ought to do something. It looked like he was going to get away.'

'It's that blasted interfering Roman!' said Dennis wearily. 'Is anyone ELSE expected to arrive, or can I go and have a bath and something to eat?'

'Salve, sire,' said Gaius, politely. 'I hope you and your lovely wife enjoyed your trip to Rome.'

'No we didn't! And unless you have something SENSIBLE to say I suggest you go STRAIGHT BACK to your MUDDY VILLAGE if you don't want me to ARREST you too!' shouted Dennis.

'Now, Dennis,' said Prunehilda. 'You mustn't be rude to Gaius. He is a PROPER Roman, after all.'

'GUARDS! I THOUGHT I TOLD YOU TO ARREST THE PEASANTS!' shouted Dennis. 'SO WHY HAVEN'T YOU?'

The guards looked at each other and shuffled their feet nervously.

'I don't think they want to arrest the peasants, because it was the peasants who rescued them from the dungeons and saved the castle, sire,' said Norman, looking nervous, 'after young Mucus did what he did, and let Yellowbeard come and take over the castle and everything.'

'Is this true?' asked Dennis.

The guards all nodded.

'And has my darling son been LYING?' asked Dennis.

The guards all nodded again, and while this was going on, Mucus had quietly slipped away from Prunehilda and was just tiptoeing off when . . .

'MUCUUUUS!' shouted Dennis, again.

shuffling feet

Looking nervous

Tiptoeing off

Chapter Twenty-one

THE END (REALLY)
OF A STONKINGLY GOOD
ADVENTURE

There was an AWFUL lot of shouting.

Dennis shouted at Mucus and Prunehilda shouted
at Dennis and Boris and Lucretia shouted at Sinus
and everyone shouted at everyone else, so while they
were all busy shouting, we slipped out of the castle
and headed home. Denzel bounded ahead of us, happily
unaware of how close he'd come to being boiled in
spices and served up with apple sauce.

And as we walked back down the hill, I thought

about how happy I was that we were heading home to Little Soggy-in-the-Mud, which thanks to us was safe once more from bloodthirsty pirates and spoilt posh boys. And I suddenly felt pleased that although we were poor we were happy, because it seemed to me that rich people just argued a lot and were mostly NOT happy.

Much later, as we all sat contentedly chatting together under the Old Oak Tree, Verucca said, 'Sorry Mucus turned out to be such a two-faced twonkhead, Rubella.'

US All feeling happy that we're not rich

'Cheers, Verucca Stupidface,' said Rubella. 'He was, wasn't he? **AND** he was a **WELL** boring wimp, too. I'm not giving up, though. I'm still going to leave this borin' pointless village one day, and have loads of money and posh clothes and live in a fancy castle. Or I might become a pirate. The clothes are **WELL** nice,' she said, flicking her hair and grinning as she got up to go. 'You coming, Gert?' she said.

'Er – no thanks, Rubes,' said Gert. 'I think I'll stay here with Urk.'

Urk blushed right to the roots of his spiky hair.

Rubella off to be a pirate
(or something) →

← URK –
all embarrassed

'What?' he said. 'There *IS* something on my face isn't there? Is it pirate sick or something? Why are you all smiling at me?'

The next day, as we all woke up to a happy pirate-free morning in Little Soggy-in-the-Mud, a small rabbit with one ear and a three-legged hedgehog ambled sleepily out from under a pile of leaves, and at the same time, my mum started screaming from our hovel. **'WILFRED! SEDRIC! COME HERE NOW! THERE'S A SNAKE IN THE BED!'**

Snake in bed!

PULL ON YOUR WELLIES — THINGS ARE ABOUT TO GET MUDDY!